Wit's End

ALSO BY SANDRA SHAMAS
Sandra Shamas: A Trilogy of Performances

Wit's End

by Sandra Shamas

THE MERCURY PRESS

The publisher gratefully acknowledges the financial assistance of the Canada Council for the Arts, the Ontario Arts Council, and the Ontario Tax Credit Program. The publisher further acknowledges the financial support of the Government of Canada through the Department of Canadian Heritage's Book Publishing Industry Development Program (BPIDP) for our publishing activities.

Edited by Beverley Daurio
Composition and page design by Beverley Daurio
Cover photograph by Kevin Hewitt

Printed and bound in Canada
Printed on acid-free paper

1 2 3 4 5 06 05 04 03 02

Canadian Cataloguing in Publication Data:
Shamas, Sandra
Wit's end
ISBN 1-55128-097-3
I. Title II. Series
PS8576.I32S97 2001 C811'.54 C2001-902999-3
PR9199.3.M4564S97 2001

The Mercury Press
Box 672, Station P, Toronto, Ontario Canada M4S 2Y4
www.themercurypress.ca

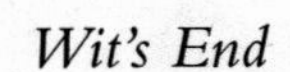

Wit's End

There's a saying in the world, and it goes like this:

"Oh, one day we're going to laugh about this."

Well... this is that day.

What happened was this: I wrote and directed and performed and produced three two-hour, one-woman shows in a seven-year period. Now, you have to understand that wasn't what I was gonna do with my life, you know what I mean?

When I was a teenager and I was called into career counselling in high school, I didn't go into the guidance counsellor's office and talk to the ancient woman behind the desk and say to her,

"Okay, like, okay, like, what I'm thinking of doing, okay, okay, all right, like what I really want to do is stand, but then mostly I would like to talk."

And she, of course, being really, really ancient, and supportive, says,

"Fabulous. We'll put you in an Arts Program."

No, that didn't happen.

Basically I did whatever I could do to keep body

and soul together. I did hundreds of different kinds of things to make money, and you know, my mandate was: three squares and a cot, three square meals and a cot. And I managed to do some pretty interesting things and through some luck and some serendipity, and in one case, through somebody I was sleeping with— that was the eighties— I got to do some fairly interesting things.

And when I turned thirty, I had my "shit or get off the pot" moment. Now I don't know if anybody here has turned thirty yet... Yeah? But for me, when that happened, I knew I could not do what I had been doing, but I didn't know what to do. And when you're in that place, you can't talk to anybody about it in real terms.

You can't say to your friends,

"I don't know what to do. I'm not sure what I'm doing. What should I do?"

And you know, they're getting ready to go to jobs they fuckin' hate, and they're thinking,

"Shut the hell up!"

I knew the answer wasn't out in the world, and so rather than go out, I went in, and I asked my Self— I asked my own Voice like a prayer—

"What do I do? You've got to help me out, I

don't even know what I do, you've gotta help me out!"

And the Voice said:

"Stand on stage and tell the truth."

Oh, perfect: nobody is ever going to pay money to hear the truth!

But I had no choice. I had no choice. I put a little show together, and I went and did my show, and I told my truth as best as I knew it, and two women told two other women, and two other women told two other women, and then they told a man. I did my first show, and it was wondrous and I loved it.

When I was done, I asked the Voice,

"What do I do now?"

And the Voice said,

"Well, do number two."

And I did the second show, I got better at my craft, I got better at producing, which is literally putting my money where my mouth is, I got better at being me onstage, and then when the second show was over, I said,

"What do I do?"

And the Voice said,

"Three. Must I count for you, stupid woman, get on it!"

So I did the third show, and I did the third show at the Winter Garden Theatre, and it was wondrous, and when the third show was finished, I said to the Voice, "So, what do I do, what do I do now?"

And there was silence! I had never heard silence from the Voice. And I panicked immediately. It was like falling from grace.

I thought, "Oh, I'm asking the Voice at the wrong time, I'll ask the Voice later. I'll ask the Voice later."

Four o'clock in the morning, panicking, waking up, going,

"What do I do with my life?"

Silence.

I didn't even want to address it. I didn't even want to address what that silence meant. Was it that our time together, this process, this relationship, this conversation, was coming to an end? I didn't even want to know. I didn't want to look at it. I didn't want to even think that what I was doing was coming to an end. I was terrified. I just completely frittered around; I frittered around, I didn't know what to do; I was wasting my energy.

It was at that exact moment in time I got an invitation from an American producer, who said,

"Would you like to bring your first show to San Francisco?"

And I screamed, "Yes! Damn you, yes, that's what I'll do."

I answered with my head, not my heart, and I just took all my panic and my fear and denial, and I aimed it at San Francisco, where they know nothing of panic, fear and denial. They live on a fucking fault line!

So venues are rented and tickets are printed and I've got my immigration papers going and I'm waiting and waiting and waiting to get into the United States. American Immigration will not allow me into the United States, five days into the performance schedule. Tickets are re-routed and people are inconvenienced and I am sitting a tortured five days here in Toronto, waiting... waiting. Finally, I'm allowed in, I'm flown to San Francisco, limo-d to the theatre. I stand on stage and I perform. Within three performances, every newspaper in the San Francisco Bay area goes on strike for five weeks.

I'm fucked! There's no way to advertise, I will not be reviewed, there's no way to get the word out. I am there for every day of five weeks, and every day of five weeks, I am *the* most grateful Canadian in the world. I am so glad to be Canadian. I am so grateful to have been born on this side of the forty-ninth parallel. 'Cause the United States of America basically terrifies me. I don't know where the floor is, I don't know where the ceiling is, and the walls are moving back and forth. I have no sense of place there, and I don't know what the hell's going on. For instance, if you pull up to the toll booth, and you don't pay the guy the buck, does he shoot you? He's wearing a gun. I need an answer to that question, do you understand?

Finally I leave San Fiasco, as it becomes known, and I fly back. When we land at Pearson I am crying, I am so grateful to be home...

We get off the airplane, I am kissing the ground! I got my big ass in the air and I am kissing the ground. I'm virtually necking with my Health Card all the way home.

Oh, baby, I'm going to get sick so soon, oh, yeah!

Maybe something with a machine!

I come home, I make the choice to obey my Voice.

I say to my husband, Frank, "I just need to stop working. I don't know what that is, I just know that I have to stop."

He said, "Okay, do what you need to do."

So, I declared a sabbatical. A sabbatical is when you take a year off after having worked seven. So, it worked perfectly, right? I'd worked seven, I was going to take a year off, and towards that end, when theatre companies would invite me to perform, to bring my show to their theatres, I would simply say,

"Thank you, I'm flattered. I'm taking a year off. I've declared a sabbatical."

And they laughed.

They did.

I thought I was telling people who would understand, and say things that were... encouraging? No. They said things like,

"Sabbatical?! From what?! It doesn't look like you do anything up there!"

You know, granted that what I'm doing up here doesn't look like ditch-digging, but there is an effort, you know? And you know what? The creative process, generally speaking, is misunderstood. Because the creative process doesn't "look" like anything. No, the creative process looks like a woman sitting catatonic in a chair, picking her nose, rolling the snot thoughtfully between her fingers, and then flicking it somewhere.

I could understand their confusion.

So I say to Frank, "You know, my eye wants to wander. I don't know exactly what that means, it's just... my eye just wants to travel without having a car stop it, or a building in the way. I just want to be in a place where I can see for as far as I want."

And he said, "Well, what are you thinking?"

I said, "Well, you know, whenever we visit Bill and Sherry (our friends, they live on a dairy farm), it's like that, like space. I need *space*."

I said, "You know, maybe we should think about buying a little cottage, or a little farm, or something; you know, we'd have a city house, and a country place. What do you think?"

He said, "Well, okay, let's look."

And I said, "We could look in Bill and Sherry's neighbourhood. If we found something, and we liked it, then we'd have instant neighbours," which is smart thinking for city folk, let me tell you.

"And," I said, "if we do find something, we'll also know the way," which is also important.

Well, sure enough, we go, and we're looking in their neighbourhood. We find a little farm. We buy it. So the sabbatical has been declared, the farm has been purchased, and little renovations are going on. Nothing big... you know, we're just taking the bathroom out of the kitchen. It's a decision I've never regretted.

I have one more contractual obligation. It is in Ottawa, at the National Arts Centre, in April of 1995. I go, ostensibly for the last work that I will ever do.

When I get to Ottawa, I commence having a series of anxiety-driven nightmares. Now, I don't know if anybody here, when you're worried about a particular thing, you have the same dream. Do you know what I mean? Like, when I'm worried about money, I have my "Waitress Dream." Yeah, that's how it shows up in my subconscious.

So, in the dream, I'm a waitress again at The Bamboo Gardens, the home of fine Canadian and Chinese cuisine in Sudbury, Ontario. I'm in my present-day consciousness but I'm in *that* uniform again, with the plum sauce fuckin' dripping off it. I'm there again, and only *my* section fills up. And I'm panicking, and then everybody starts banging on the table with their cutlery. I don't know what to do. I panic, and I'm overwhelmed. I turn to look for help from the other waitresses but nobody wants to help me, because they're mad, because only my section has people in it.

Fuck you!

I always wake up out of that dream thinking,

"The minute I get money I'm buying a new dream, that's all there is to it."

The first dream in Ottawa, the first dream, I am in a ballroom. I am in a vast ballroom that is so beautiful. The walls are literally glimmering, and everyone in the room is beautiful, and really happy to be there, and so am I. I'm amongst these people, and I'm very happy. As I am turning to speak with the tall man that's standing to my left, I blink, and when I open my eyes, he's gone. And then I look, and everybody else is gone, and I am the only one in this vast, beautiful room. And when I wake up out of the dream, I am unnerved. Like my skin's not on right, and I'm trying to figure it out.

And as I'm brushing my teeth, which is usually when I do all my best self-analysis, I think,

"Well, maybe the ballroom is the theatre. Maybe that's it. And maybe because I won't be performing any more, and I won't be with my audience any more, and I always loved that, I love doing what I do, and

I'm not going to be doing that any more. Maybe that's it. That must be it. That has to be it."

I placate myself with this explanation, but I know something is wrong.

Second dream comes, two or three nights later. I am standing on rock, as far as the eye can see. I am standing alone on a vast amount of rock. Without notice, all the rock in my vision falls six thousand feet, save for what's underneath my own. Where I was standing on level ground, I am now standing atop a six-thousand foot monolith. If I move forward or back or side-to-side, I will plummet to my death.

This dream I come up out of screaming. I wake up screaming. I have never done that; that in itself terrifies me.

I get up out of the bed. And I am yelling and pointing at the bed,

"It's just a dream! It's just a dream!"

It's not good. Something is definitely wrong. I can sense it, but I have no idea what it is.

Now I don't want to go to sleep.

I'm too scared to go to sleep, but I can't stay up long enough.

The third dream comes, and it just keeps repeating, over and over,

"Frank's going to divorce you, Frank's going to divorce you."

This dream puts me over.

I am crying, hysterically. I call my brother, Michael, who lives in Ottawa.

I say, "Michael, can you please talk to me for a minute? I'm so scared, I don't know what's going on, I can't even tell you..." I'm crying; I'm blathering; I'm hysterical.

He says, "Okay, okay, listen to me. What's going on?"

So I tell him about the dreams: the ballroom, the falling stone, the standing alone, Frank's going to divorce me, all told with a voice choked with hysteria.

And Michael listens very carefully, very patiently. Then he says to me, "Now, listen, Sandra. How many people in the world do you know who volunteer to stop working? How many? None, that's how many. You know why? Because not working creates stress. People are hard-wired into the validation that work gives them, and when that stops, people become very, very upset."

He said, "When was the last time you didn't work?"

I said, "Mike, you know I've always worked."

He said, "Exactly. Exactly. You've decided to stop working, and now you're creating stress, and you're working it out in your subconscious."

A little smile crosses my face. "Oh, you're a smarty-pants. Mr. Pants," I said, "but Mike, what about the Frank's-going-to-divorce-me dream? What does that mean? What's wrong? Something's wrong!"

He said, "Now, listen. How long do you have left in Ottawa?"

I said, "I have two days left."

And he said, "Frank's in Montreal. How long's he got?"

I said, "Two weeks."

He said, "And then?"

I said, "And then Frank is going to come home."

He says lovingly, "Yeah, and you're going to go to the farm and you're going to have fun and it's going to be okay."

Okay. "You are wise in the ways of the subconscious, Mike."

I finished April the 29th, 1995. I flew home April the 30th, 1995.

At 11:36 p.m., according to the digital clock, the phone rings.

It is my husband, Frank, calling from Montreal.

He says, "We've gotta talk."

I said, "What, now?"

He says, "I'm not coming home."

Big heat crosses my chest. "Ummm... I'm listening..."

He says, "I'm not coming home ever. I'm never coming home."

I said, "Could we please talk about this in person?"

He said, "Okay. I have a day off tomorrow. I'll fly to Toronto."

I hung up the phone, numb.

And the Voice, so long silent, says,

"This is a good thing."

I don't remember sleeping, I don't remember waking. I dressed, I drove to the airport, I picked up my husband. We drove wordlessly back to the house. We sat down at the kitchen table.

His first words were, "I want a divorce."

I said, "You have to give me a chance to think about this, 'cause you've been thinking about this a long time. I've had twelve hours."

He said, "Sandra, I have nothing left to give you. I want a divorce."

I said, "I don't like the way things are going either. Please, there must be something we can do!"

He says, "No, I want a divorce, and I've made a flight out of Toronto in an hour."

The Voice says,

"This is a good thing."

And even I can see it is a completely non-negotiable situation.

I simply nod.

"Okay."

I check my watch for the time. I drive him back to the airport... like a fuckin' nutbar! And that's virtually the last time I ever saw him. It was May the 1st, 1995, first day of sabbatical, and I was about to be divorced. No wonder they call it... May Day.

I went home and I stood perfectly still. It didn't elude me that I had written three bodies of work that included the relationship with this man, and even if I wanted to work, the emotional validity of that work was gone. I stood perfectly still, and I just felt waves of shame crashing on me, like shame, smashing, smashing on me, and then the undertow of failure. I have never been in a place like this in my life. It's awful. I stood perfectly still, and I didn't tell anybody because I was so ashamed.

That was May the 1st. On May the 4th, I received notice of litigation. The American producer I'd been working with in San Francisco was preparing to sue me to compensate himself for the five days American Immigration would not allow me into the country.

And then, I started my period.

Thank you, Jesus!

Oh, yeah, it was a big week!

I called my brother, Michael, who no longer has the job of family oracle. I was crying hysterically with him, I was hysterical, I was screaming hysterically, and when I was trying to catch my breath I could hear my brother whisper into my ear,

"I love you. I love you."

Michael and I would speak to each other every day for a year. And every day for a year, Michael would find some way to tell me he loved me. I love that man.

When I hung up the phone from Mike, the phone rings ten minutes later.

It's my friend Maria calling, chirping, "Hey, you, I haven't heard from you since Ottawa. How's it going?"

Beat.

"Maria... Maria, Frank and I are getting a divorce."

She says, questioningly, "What's that, sweetheart?"

I said, "Frank and I are separating, and we're getting a divorce!"

She says, with more gravity, "Sandra, what the hell are you talking about?"

I said, "Frank left me, and now we're getting a divorce!"

She says, matter-of-factly, "When did this happen?"

"On May the 1st."

She says, almost angry, "Why didn't you tell me?"

I cried, "Because I didn't want you to leave me, too."

I just thought everybody I loved would line up behind him and go. I didn't know. I forgot. I made a mistake. I forgot that when people truly love one another, they do so unconditionally. I forgot that when women love one another, they love one another unconditionally.

You see, in the Wild, Wild World of Women, when there's bad news, it just goes out like a hue and cry:

"One of us is down!"

And they come. And they come and they put their Astro wagons in a circle.

Everyone's on the phone: "Oh, my God, did you hear? Did you hear? Oh, my God! Well, you know what? Let's get going. And bring that pimento loaf. I hear she's not eating!"

They came by phone, by foot, by fax. And they came, they came, they came, and they all came to my house, and we sat down at the kitchen table, and the first question always is:

"How are you?"

"I'm not good. I'm not good."

And they would hold me, and I would cry, and they would cry, and we would cry. And then: kleenex, much nose blowing, and sniffling.

And then we'd have a snack.

Oh, girls love a snack! It's the only reason we go to a funeral. The snack makes way for the second question, which always is:

"Sandra, honey, was there somebody else?"

In my naïveté: "I asked him, and he said no!" And I believed him.

You know, a man— a man said to me, "Uh, Sandra, are you a new kind of stupid? Men don't jump, dear, unless they've got somewhere soft to land!"

It is at this point that everybody shares, because everybody's life blows up, and you've got that story, and you've saved it for such a festive occasion. So each in turn tells her story, and we all support with kleenex or snacks, and then we'd have a big old communal cry. And then: more nose blowing.

And then somebody'd say, "You know, dear, oh, I could go for something sweet. Oh, but I couldn't eat the whole thing. I'll split it with you."

Have you ever seen two women on a pie? One pie, two forks. There's a silent agreement as to who goes in first, and she just fuckin' reefs into her. When she's finished, the second one says, "Oh, now look at that. Let me just clean up that edge." It is in this way that they agree to go around the entire pie.

Now there is the issue of the last piece. One will say to the other, "No, go ahead, no, I'm full, no, go ahead."

But she's thinking, "That cow just ate half a pie! And now she's going to rob me of the last piece!"

The sweet thing makes way for the hard question. The hard question is on everyone's mind, but only one woman will ask it. She is the one who always asks the hard questions:

"Well, you must have seen it coming. You were there the whole time. You must have seen it coming."

"Uh... uh, oh... no. I didn't see it coming."

Or did I?

I mean, you look out the window, you see rain, you know what rain is, you prepare for rain. The for sure thing you know about rain is that you cannot stop it. If it has rained every day of your life, you don't know the difference. You think rain is normal. Some days it rains less than others; some days it doesn't rain at all, which actually feels odd. I prepared for rain and I knew, I knew that there were things that were very wrong, I knew that there were things that were very very wrong, but I also knew that I could not fix them by myself. I prepared for rain, not Armageddon.

Then you've got to have a laugh. You've got to have a laugh, and it's usually delivered by the one who's seen the most life:

"Well, you know, Sandra..."— as she's digging

her underwire out of her right tit— "fuck him! He's in Montreal, is he? Well, when they separate, they can have him!"

It is in this way that women come together to support, and console, and honour the end of love. And then they go home to their lives. I was never forgotten. Somebody called every day.

Extra cheery: "Hiiii! You wake up? Whatcha wearin'?"

"Mostly just Post-Its today."

The women were unconditionally supportive. It is because of women that I am alive.

I was part of a couple, and my couple was part of a gang of couples— like a coven of couples, if you will? And when you're a couple and you hang out with other couples, every couple in the coven has an emotional investment in the continuance of each of these relationships, because they're kind of reflective of who you are, right? So, if somebody wobbles over here, *everybody* kind of goes wobbly. If somebody snaps apart, everybody goes to either end of the galaxy. And you know, in coupledom, everyone is quite convinced that their relationship is way more emotionally safe and healthy than everybody else's, as is revealed in the post-party drive home.

He says, from the driver's side, "Oh, she had a couple of drinks."

She says, arms crossed on the passenger side, "Well, if I was married to him I'd drink, too, you know."

"Well, I think she's got a problem."

"Well, I think *he's* her problem."

Silence.

He finally says, "But we're okay, though."

"Oh, yeah, we're fuckin' perfect! We just hang around with really fucked-up people."

The couples were making choices. They were making choices I think they didn't even understand themselves. Things were changing and would change forever. Their support was limited and I was grateful for that, because to be near them was to be reminded of what I was, and what I was lamenting, and for them to be near me was to address a potential no couple ever wants to address. All relationships are fragile, somewhere. The couples were as supportive as they could be, and I was grateful for it.

The men on their own... The men on their own went wonky. It's the only way I know how to describe it. These are guys I thought I knew, and now I couldn't have identified them in a line-up. Some of them were very angry. They were very angry at me— pointing and yelling angry. Some actually took the time out of their busy day to humiliate me, publicly. Somebody else came on to me. Now, here's a strategy I would never have ever predicted in a million years. You understand? My-mouth-wide-open, no-voice-coming-out kind of astonishment.

I'll try to describe how it went.

It's Sunday. It's Sunday. I've been invited to a Sunday barbecue. It's daylight, it's Canada, you know. I'm at this thing, and you understand, I'm a *mess*! I'm a fucking mess, and reality is blurring for me, do you understand? It's like the whole world is under water, and I'm squinting through all of this, trying to determine what is actually real, and I'm watching everyone at the barbecue get their plates, and load up on potato salad, and I'm standing on the periphery, and he's standing beside me, and while I'm looking on, sort of squinting at all this, I hear in my ear:

"Hey... why don't you and I go upstairs and..."

"Wha'?"

I'm so damaged, I think it's *me*— I take it on, right? I think he's asked for a glass of water, and I'm so fucked up, I've churned it into something fucking bad! So I say to him laughingly, 'cause he's my friend, I turn and say:

"Listen, I'm so fucked up, do you want to know how fucked up I am? I actually thought..."

— now I'm really laughing—

"I thought you just came on to me..."

He says,

"Um, yeah, I did."

My bottom falls out.

My eyes go straight to his wife.

I whisper, "She's right there. She's right there."

He shrugs, saying,

"Yeah, I know."

"Well, you know what, one of us loves her very, very much, and I think it's me."

Why would I do that to her?

Why would I ever do anything to her, she who was so good to me?

I felt betrayed for myself, and I felt betrayed for her. And in doing what he did, he drew a line around us that I could not step out of. I could not go to my world for consolation. As betrayed as I felt, I hung on to it, I hung on to it, I hung on to it.

I ended up having a conversation over coffee with some twenty-two-year-old guy I didn't even know, and then I lost it!

Screaming,

"I was just standing there and I didn't do anything and then he came on to me and his wife is right there and he didn't even care and what the fuck is that? I want you to explain your fucking species to me!"

He's as far back in his chair as he can get.

Scared. "I... I dunno. Okay, maybe right now it's just like you're really vulnerable, and he's just trying to help."

What is that, the male equivalent to a casserole?

Unzipping his pants, "Yeah, I heard you're sad," carefully creasing them and laying them on the back of the chair, looking down at his erection, saying, "Yeah, look what I made you. I made it myself."

Nothing says loving like something from the oven, eh?

Now, whenever I don't want to accept something, I try to reason with it. It's called a "failed relationship," so I wanted to know when it failed, like where was the point of failure? Were we just going along and then *pfft!* it failed? Or, were we failing all along? And then, in ultimately failing, did we succeed?

You know, whenever there's calamity, you think of every time there was something wrong, something calamitous that happened in your life. I sat down, and I went back through every failed relationship I have ever had. It was exhausting. And I went right back to my own genesis, to the very very first failed relationship of my whole life, which was the one that I had with my mother.

You know, if the definition of true love is to look into someone's eyes and know you will love them forever, I am sure that is what happens between a mother and a child. I loved my mother. I loved her. I didn't like her. And I'll go out on a limb and say those feelings were reciprocated. And we had a very long, and angry, and violent relationship, and I never understood it, and I tried to figure it out in my child's mind, but I never ever did. And finally, when I was seventeen, I left home to save my life.

As I am thinking of this, I hear the Voice say:

"Forgive by Wednesday. Call by Sunday."

"What?! I'm not going to forgive her, I'm not forgiving her, I'm not forgiving her, because she was mean to me the whole time. I am not forgiving her, and besides, she never called me!"

"Forgive by Wednesday. Call by Sunday."

The Voice is persistent, and it is always right.

A window of opportunity opens in this moment like never before and I see her like another woman. She is twenty-two years old, and she is being married to a man twenty years her senior through an arranged marriage. She has known him for two weeks. She will eventually leave her home and her community and be brought to Canada, to live amongst strangers, to see snow for the first time. She will live in isolation, and within ten months of her arrival, have a child in her arms. I thought, if somebody was telling me that story, I would be crying and saying, "How sad for you, and I'm so, so sorry." I saw that she had limited resources. I call it "stick soup." Whenever we needed anything from her, she'd take her "stick" and she'd say, "Come on, come on, come and get it," and she'd swirl her stick around, and whatever she made, we loved, because it came from her.

And then, when we went out into the world and we saw other people had other kinds of soup, we said, "Hey, you're supposed to be delivering this other stuff, you know."

She goes, "I don't know what you're talking about. I've never even seen that. I don't even know anything about that. I have *this*, this stick is *all* I have, and what I know, and I'm giving you everything I have."

I saw in that moment my mother was doing the best she could.

Immediately, a parallel drawn between my mother and myself, and my limited resources, in my relationship. If I had known better, I would have done better. I did not know better. When I look at the calendar, we're still in the merry month of May. Wednesday is May the 10th. That's my mother's birthday. So on that Wednesday, I forgave her, and released myself from so much anger, and so much resentment and so much bitterness. It was more like a gift to me, really.

Sunday was Mothers' Day.

I sat by the phone.

I sat by the phone.

I was sweating, I was sweating, I was panicking and crying, and I'd pick up the phone and I'd put it down.

I couldn't call her and I couldn't leave, and I was just sitting there panicking and crying, scared, really scared, like hard scared, and I didn't know what to do. So I picked up the phone and I called my brother.

"Michael. Michael. Michael, I'm gonna call her."

He says, "You're gonna call *her*?"

We know who "her" is.

I said, "Yes, I'm gonna call her."

He says, "Sandra, when was the last time you spoke to her?"

I said, "Twenty years ago."

He said, "I'm scared."

I said, "Me, too."

And he said, "Yeah, but call me after, though, eh?"

He gives me the number. I hang up from Michael and pick up the phone again.

My heart is beating so hard I can see the skin on my chest moving.

I dial the number.

Of course, I've never forgotten it in all my whole life.

Somebody else answers the phone.

I ask for her by her first name, the phone goes down on the counter, and I hear footsteps coming towards the phone. And then, the first voice of my whole life picks up the phone, and says, "Hello?"

"Mama?"

She says, "Sandra?"

I say, "Yeah, Mama, it's me."

"How are *you*?"

I said, "I'm really nervous, Mama."

She says quickly, "What are you nervous about?"

"I haven't talked to you in a long, long time."

She sobs, "I know. I think about you every day."

I said, "You do?!"

She says, "What do you think, uh? You're my daughter."

I hadn't been somebody's daughter in twenty years. And man, we cried.

And so there I am on the phone with my mom after twenty years, and I say, "Mama... Mama, I was married to a man, and he left me."

She said, "Well, I don't know. Something wrong with *him*."

If your mom says so, it's true!

I went to see her. Two days later I went to see her. In my child's mind's eye, my mother was eight-and-a-half feet tall, like a Tyrannosaurus rex, and when I got to the door, and the door opened, she is five-foot-three.

"Hey-hey-hey! You are little! I could just squeeze your head!"

It was good to go home. It was good to make peace.

Amen.

I came back to Toronto. Now, I'd been doing a fair bit of crying. Yeah, I was really applying myself. I think when you work that hard at something, you should get something for it. Now, in workshopping this show, I asked women where they liked to cry, because women love to cry, and some women have special spots that they love to cry in.

I asked the women; I didn't ask the men. I don't care.

My favourite place to cry in the whole wide

world is behind the wheel.Yes! I love to drive and cry!

Now, there's a bit of a criteria, for those of you who've never experienced the deliciousness of driving and crying.

You need a big piece of asphalt in front of you. A big hunk of the 401.You need to be in the fast lane, and you need to be going a minimum 120 K. I don't advocate speeding; I just know that this is the speed at which the tears will shudder themselves out of your eyes.

So you've got a big piece of asphalt, you're having a nice cry, everything's moving along nicely. If you just want to bump up that experience, turn on the country channel. Baby, for sure, somebody else is having a worse day than you. So you've got your snot bubble going there. You're begging for windshield wipers on the inside, you know. Oh, it's a beautiful thing.

Then I started noticing other women driving and crying.

There was one woman, in a green Safari wagon. It was the summer, she's in the fast lane, she is going mach two, and she is just hanging off her wheel, throwing down, bawling her head off. I'm driving beside her, yelling:

"Open your eyes! Open your eyes! Hey! What channel are you on?!"

Oh, yeah.

I stopped eating. I didn't care to eat. People got worried. They said things like:

"You've got to eat something. Damn it, you've got to eat something!"

"Something" became the only thing I would eat, and then I couldn't be without it. My food of preference for this event was the President's Choice Figs First Fig Newtons. Do you know them at all? Yes? Cakey, yet figgy. And you eat two, and you're full. And can we talk "regular"? It was fantastic!

And I cut my hair. I got my hair cut. Now, the rule of hairdressing, as you know, is, go to your own kind. She who has your hair, knows your hair; and she has an investment in what you look like when you leave. A woman with straight hair could give a shit what I look like. My hairdresser, Claire, has curly, curly hair, bubbly curly hair.

So I sit down. She puts this big bib on me.

I say, "Claire, take it off."

She gasps, "Uh! Are you sure?" Thick British accent.

I say, "Yeah! I'm sure."

She says, "When you cut your hair, it's as if you leave your past behind."

"Fig Newton, Claire? I'm leaving a lot behind."

Now we get to the divorce, and the happy division of assets. I stopped asking members of the audience "Who here has been divorced?", because nobody puts up their hand, leading me to believe I am the only one in Canada. That's fine. I'm a divorcée. Divorcée. Divorcée. I think there's an *accent aigu* on that.

The happy division of assets is simply that. Whatever you have amassed during the lifetime of your relationship is somehow divided. I say "somehow," because this particular arena can become fairly nasty. I have heard that some people display not such a nice part of themselves during this process. In fact, I have heard that some people invite Satan to come up from Hell and mediate the event. Apparently, the Great Horned One can be very diplomatic.

In my case, if conflict is contact, we had virtually none. Within two phone calls, we had divided everything. We had a house in the country and a half-ton; we had a house in the city and a Volvo. I wanted the half-ton, and the country house went with it. He got the Volvo and the city house. I got my money; he got his. I got my stuff; he got his; like, straight down the middle, like surgery.

I needed a lawyer, of course, because I can't do everything— as it turns out. I asked Sherry if she knew anybody in the country, and she says, "Well, you know, I know a lawyer, but I don't know if he does divorce. He's a really great guy, he did work for us, and we were very happy with what he did. In fact, he accepted a load of manure as payment."

You know, that's a man, to me. His name is Warren. I asked him if he'd ever thought of changing his last name to Peace, and specializing in divorce. He didn't laugh, which was how I knew he was a lawyer, so I hired him immediately.

I needed a litigation lawyer as well. I was up to my tits in lawyers. I needed a litigation lawyer, you know, to deal with this pending litigation, and a human being showed up with litigation abilities. This man, he was a human being first.

He said, "You know, Sandra, prior to Free Trade, Americans really didn't try to come across the border and sue, because they weren't very successful. But now that Free Trade is in place, many Americans come across and successfully litigate against Canadians."

Well, bully for them.

He said, "If we go to court, it will be a very long, drawn-out, and expensive process. If we settle out of court, that means we will negotiate back and forth on an amount of money that you will, eventually, pay. And when that number is arrived upon, is there a way for you to philosophically accept this expenditure?"

Wow. You know, that just set it on its side for me. Prior to that, I felt like a victim of this man. The first image that flashed in my head was writing out a cheque to an exterminator. I thought of it as getting debugged. Like, yes, I have an infestation, an awful infestation here, and if I write you this cheque, will you get rid of it? And he did. And, yay, it was done! Hallelujah, get out of my life.

So, I had lawyers on the boil, they're all boiling away, I didn't have much to do after that, so I just took the half-ton, I backed it up to the house, I loaded it up, pulled up the tailgate, said goodbye to my house, said goodbye to the city, and I headed for the hills.

I named the farm "Wit's End," because that's where I was. You know, I felt like I was being banished from my whole life; anything that I had worked for, put any kind of investment in, was absolutely gone from my sight. My relationship was gone, my work was gone, and my city-world was gone. I was the only thing left standing, and I could barely recognize myself.

I said to Sherry, "Sherry, women don't live alone on farms, Sherry, they just don't!"

She said, "Well, you know what, honey, I don't think you have a choice."

I said, "But what if there's a medical emergency?"

She said, "Well, if it's any consolation, they can land a helicopter in your front yard."

Now, the farm itself is a house, and a barn, and the house and the barn sit on a piece of property that is one hundred and twenty-three acres. The fifty that are around the house and barn are presently in hay, the middle fifty are hardwood forest, mostly maple, and the bottom twenty-three acres hold a twelve-acre lake that's thirty-five feet deep. It's pretty where I live.

Somebody asked me, "Did you purchase a rural property because you were raised in a rural landscape?"

I said, "No, I was raised in a lunar landscape." Which is Sudbury, Ontario, 1960-anything. Inco, that fine corporate citizen, basically smelted anything green off the fuckin' face of that place.

When I was a kid I remember my dad telling a story once at supper, that if the paint on your vehicle was bubbling because of the shit that was falling out of the sky, then you could call Inco and they would take your vehicle and repaint it for you. There's that nasty pollution problem taken care of, there you go. And then they got so much pressure from the environmentalists, they built the Super Stack, and started painting cars in Parry Sound.

No, I wasn't raised in Nature. I hardly knew what my own nature was.

So I moved out to the farm. The very first thing I noticed is how quiet it is. It is skull-crushingly quiet. It is so quiet, all you can hear is the bullshit in your own head! And I had no shortage of it. It was like tuning a short-wave radio from hell.

Like, you're tuning, and you hit the who-do-you-think-you-are channel. Then you keep tuning, until you hit the what-the-hell-do-you-think-you're-doing channel, or my favourite, the no-one's-ever-going-to-love-you channel. Shut the fuck up!

The second thing I noticed, pretty much the same day, is how dark it gets at night. It is *so* dark. They are serious about black. It's like a black I've never even seen, it's like a puddingy, thicky, puddingy black; it's like so fuckin' black, okay, when it went black, it turned every window in the house into a mirror! Walking through the house that night, I suddenly saw someone following me. And I screamed! It was just my reflection, but that's no way to get to the kitchen, let me tell you.

And last, but not least— if you hear a sound, something *makes it*. So my ears were the size of an elephant's. I'm getting ready to go to bed, I'm on the second floor of my house, and if you look off into the distance, against the road, you can see the silhouette of the Group of Seven trees. Group of Seven trees look like this: all their limbs are on one side. Hydro makes them. Yeah. It's a perfectly good tree and then Hydro comes along, lops off all the limbs on one side, making them Group of Seven trees.

I'm getting ready to go to bed, so I get into bed, and I start tucking my ears in with me, and I'm propped up, 'cause there's no fuckin' way I'm lying down! And as I'm lying there, and it's so black, I think of that expression,

"It was so dark you couldn't see your hand in front of your face," and I'm experimenting with it, and I boink myself in the eye.

Ow!

Now I have one eye closed— like it matters.

So as I'm lying there, or propped up there, more or less, I hear a terrible screeching, choking sound.

I bring up the big Rolodex of sounds:

Choo choo?

No.

Piano?

No.

Sound of something losing its life?

Yeah.

I make the choice at that moment not to run out and save it. Because while something is dying, something else is *dining*.

This is the sound of Nature shopping, apparently.

And it takes forever for something to die. It was

going on and on and on. Finally, and I never thought I'd hear *me* say, "Fuckin' die, already!"

So I'm lying there in the black, and it's the perfect moment to start The Movie of My Life!

So there it goes, every memory, every nine years' worth of memories, every look, every glance, every word, every touch, every la la la, la la la la, and I would watch, I would cry, and then I'd fall asleep

And then, I'd wake up like I'd been touched by electricity.

Jolt awake! Stare into black.

Feverish, "Where am I?"

Revelation. "I'm on the farm," and cry 'til I fall asleep.

Jolt awake, "Where am I?"

"Oh, I'm on the farm."

That went on for months

I was looking good!

I had no idea how bad it was until I got my driver's license photograph. When I looked at the photo, I was shocked.

I said, "This woman has been set on fire and put out with an axe!" Man. I still have it as a happy memento of those times.

Now, I had never made my own home. I'd never made a home for myself. I had taken all of my talent and my enthusiasm and my ability and put it into the "We," for "Us, Our," and when it came time for "Me" making my own home, I found myself strangely still, like inert, almost, and I realized that I will work harder and longer and more cheerfully on the behalf of others than I will work on my own, that I will happily do for others the very things that I need to do for myself.

And when I understood this, I was saddened by it. I thought, this is pathetic. I mean, I am not even on my own side.

And I thought, "Sandra, if you are not on your own side, who is? And, who wants to be on the side of somebody who isn't on their own side?"

Having never made my own home, I simply let the environment dictate to me. I would wake up when it got light, I would make coffee, I would sit at the kitchen table and I would look at the fields. When it got dark, I'd go to bed. I would wake up when it got light, I would make coffee, and I would sit... and if it got cold, I'd go over to the heat register and turn it up. When I got tired of standing near the heat register, I'd sit down, eat two Fig Newtons. When it got dark, I'd go to bed.

The farm is on a piece of land called the Escarpment, and the Escarpment used to be an ancient sea, and I found little fossils in the garden, sea shells embedded in sandstone, and I put them on the windowsill in front of me. And I remember one day looking out, and looking at the fields, and looking at these sea shells, and how extraordinary the thought was that this was all once under water, and how long ago that was, and I thought, geez, that's amazing, and as I looked up, I felt as if the land was looking back and laughing at me. Laughing at me, going:

"Hey! Hey you, human in the window! Yeah, you! Are you sad? Awwwwww... Hey, you see that little sea shell in front of you? It was sad, too. Then it died!"

In that moment I understood that the land is infinite, it is eternal, and I am a snap of the fingers to the land. In the timescape of the land, I am maybe half a snap; we are all a snap of the fingers to the land. I thought, "Oh, my God, I'm finite! I had no idea." I thought, you know, "If I've got a limited amount of time, I'd better get my shit together."

So I called the septic man. You want to know about shit, go to the top.

I'm on a septic system, and I didn't know where it was. I mean, I was just flushing with the hope that it was going away from the house. And it's under ground, of course, so it all looks the same, the lawn, it all looks the same, grass looks like bug looks like twig, I don't know. So I invited him to come on the land and he came, and we were walking around the house and talking and walking, and suddenly he stops and goes:

"Whoa whoa whoa whoa... there she is, right there." And he digs into the dirt with the toe of his boot.

That's how men point in the country, by the way.

I said, "That's who right where?"

He said, "That's where the opening for your septic system is, right there!"

I said, "How do you know that?"

He said, "Cleaned 'er out myself, three year ago."

"You are a god to me," I said. "Listen, is it going to be enough for me?"

He said, "You could put a family of five on that one."

I said, "You know, that's good news, 'cause I'm doing a fig thing right now."

So I found out where my septic bed was. I didn't plant a Buick there or anything. I ordered a wood stove, and I had it installed in the kitchen. From the name "wood" stove, I got some wood delivered, and they delivered the wood in the yard next to the stump. Now, it was just a stump before, but suddenly, with the wood next to it, I realized, "Oho ho ho! This is where they split the wood." Hello. I thought, you know, I can split wood. I'm kind of a Dr. Quinn, medicine woman, I can split wood. So I went out and I bought a splitting axe, which is basically a sharpened anvil on a stick.

Okay, I realized now I should've got the instructional video. Wood comes in tubes called "logs." If you want to split a log, you take a log and then you put it on the stump on its end, and let it go. It should stay. If it doesn't, just shimmy it around until it does, then let it go. It should stay. This could take hours. If it got dark, I'd go in. Start fresh in the morning. Finally I got one to stand on its own.

Okay, now, I have seen men split wood, only on

TV. They swagger as they walk towards the log, then there's the full-arm extension, lifting the axe over the head, and then the hands come together as the axe actually hits the wood, and then splits it.

There's no fucking way I could do that. The first time I lifted the axe over my head, it continued until it rested on the ground behind me, pinning me in a back bend. So, I decided I'd just choke up on it, and planted the axe in the log, and then I couldn't get it out. That was the day I decided to burn them whole! You put in enough paper, shit burns. Who's going to come by? The Wood Police? I don't think so.

Now, to get to my house, you have to go up a very big hill. I call it "The Widowmaker." It's like a two-tiered event, this thing, and well, that fall was very, very cold, and it rained, and froze quickly, and I only had the half-ton with two-wheel drive. I backed down that hill so many times, thinking, "Oh, we're not even into winter yet. How am I going to get up to the house?"

And so I went down the road and talked to Sherry's husband, Bill.

I said, "Bill, what am I going to do? Should I just go out and buy something four-wheel drive? 'Cause I can."

He says, "No, no." He kicks the tire. "That's a good truck! You just need some weight in the back. Get yourself some cement block."

I said, "Ah, phew! Thanks, Bill. Of course. Cement block. Let's go get some cement block."

Where do you get cement block? Oh, I know? I'll surf the Web. Ce-men-t Bl-ock. No web site. Under construction. So I got it into my head it had to be square, and heavy. So I was at Home Hardware, and I noticed they have bags of sand, and they were square, and heavy. So I bought ten sixty-six-pound bags of sand.

I know *now* it is too much. I didn't know. I was going with the half-ton truck, so that's how much you have to put in the back.

Anyway, I buy all this sand and then they give me the receipt, and they said at the cash, "Okay, drive around into the yard at the back and pick up the sand."

So I drive around the back, and in the yard is this really little guy. He's like, a young guy, his coat's wide open, it's freezing outside, and he's not old enough to wear gloves, apparently, so he shoves his fists up into his sleeves. He's got no scarf. His neck's all red. He's freezing out there.

So I go over and I say, "Hi. Listen, here's my receipt, I bought some sand."

He says, "Yeah, it's right there," gesturing with one of his handless arms.

Uh-huh.

I look at the sand, I look at the truck. I look at the sand. I look at the truck. I look at the sand and I realize there's no way I can lift six-hundred-and-sixty pounds of sand. I decide to use my feminine wiles, and I say, in my best girly voice:

"Um, excuse me, could you help me? Could you put them in there, 'cause I'm not very strong."

Suddenly, he's a man of action. He went, "Sure."

Okay, in my life, I have never done the jiggly thing to get a guy to do something for me. I always thought it was too manipulative to do that. I'm here to tell you, it works like a fuckin' charm. Apparently, all you have to do is pretend you're mostly cartilage. Yeah. I think it's the bones men fear. Course, I could have popped a wheelie now with the truck, I had so much fuckin' sand in the back. We are not going to even discuss the fine gas mileage I got that year.

One of the things I brought with me from the city to the country was my city arrogance. The city arrogance that lets you believe that everything in the city is hip and smooth and smart and cool, and everything in the country is dumb and dumb and dumb!

You know, when you walk on land, land is uneven, so the first thing you have to do when you walk on land is look down. Then you have to pick up your foot and make a choice as to where to put it. If you want to move forward, you have to do that again— make a choice and put it down. Choice is one of the fundamental building-blocks of creativity, so when you are walking and making a choice with every step, you're in creative flow. In the city, everything is smooth, so you don't have to look down, ever; you always look up. You're so confident everything is just smooth in front of you, and all your attitude goes into your head. Which is why city folk look extra stupid in the country. Yeah, 'cause they're walking. They don't look down. They trip. They stop. They look back to blame someone. And they do it all again. Myself included.

I had an apple tree on the land, and it was dead, and I invited a woodsman named Ray to come on the land and cut it down. I was going to burn it in the wood stove. Not whole— I was going to cut it up into bite-size pieces.

And so Ray came on the land. He had two chain saws with him, a sixteen-inch Stihl, and a Husqvarna he called "The Big Girl." This thing had her own house, you understand? It was like a trailer, a fuckin' Husqvarna trailer.

Anyway, so he's out there cutting the tree down, and I see he's taking a smoke break, so I run out to say "Hi," 'cause he's another human being.

I said, "Hey, Ray, how's it going?"

"Yeah. Okay."

I'm trying to start a conversation, and I say, "So, listen, Ray, how often do you get into the city?"

He says, "Brampton?"

I said, "No, no. God. Toronto."

He says, pondering a moment, "Oh. Maybe..." and spreads out the five fingers on one hand.

I said, "Five times a week?"

He says, "In my life."

I said, "Oh, my God, where do you go if you need a cappuccino?"

He looked sidelong at me and then away, and in that moment, I realized I would've gotten away easier if I'd just shown the man my ass.

"I have to go in now, Ray. It turns out I'm an asshole!"

Oh, man, I winced for weeks. Weeks. I'd be doing the dishes, and suddenly I'd remember what I'd said, and I'd have to go make a sound to make the sting go away; or a sudden movement works as well.

So I realized I had a lot to learn. Tolerance was on the top of my list. My first lesson in tolerance came by way of a man in my neighbourhood. I have a long driveway that comes into my home. This man is a racist, sexist, homophobic, white supremacist, and... I like him very much. Because he has a snow plough. From this man I learned a very important life lesson, which is: Fight the fight that's in front of you. Get this done. Don't be shilly-shallying, dilly-dallying out there, because if you don't get this done, then they will find your bloated body in the spring. I needed this man, and I respected him for that need. Am I ever going to talk to him about anything that isn't white snow? Not on your fuckin' life, no!

I realized very quickly that I'm the kind of person who needs an inordinate amount of attention.

Unfortunately, I was the only one out there to give it to me. It turns out I'm really not that attentive. I'm also slightly whiney. It's a bad combo.

I would have days, I called them "Days of Grace." The fact that I had nowhere to go, and nothing to do, and no responsibility, and enough money to pay for my expenses, was a most exhilarating and liberating feeling. It was: I can do anything I want. On days like that, I felt I could do anything. I would roam around, and I would discover stuff. I started just having fun, I felt... a sense of elation, really.

And if somebody called from the city, asking,

"Hey, you, what are you doing way out there?"

I'd go,

"Oh! It's so great! Okay, listen, I ate about three Fig Newtons already, and, like, I must have got about five hours sleep, maybe not all together, but like, total. And then last night, in the middle of the night, I heard coyote crossing the land!"

She goes, "Oh, my God, Sandra! Coyote in Canada?!"

I go, "Yeah, there's coyote in Canada."

I don't know if you've ever experienced coyote; when they move, they yip. Yep, "Yip yip, yip yip yip, yap yip." Coyote talk. They're just talking to one another, like, "Nice fur, good paws," stuff like that, you know.

And she says, "Oh, my God, oh, my God! Weren't you terrified?"

"No. They cannot open the door. They cannot start the truck."

Oh, yip yip, yeee, get in the back!

What? Oh, too much sand?

Yeah. Best to walk.

And then, there's the other side of the coin. On a day like that, the fact that I had nowhere to go and nothing to do, no responsibility, and the fact that I had money made it colder.

I would start imploding. The fact that I could look out a window and see nothing was just more like a reflection as to how incredibly alone I was, and how I felt. I felt it to the core of my being, and I would be so sad. I would cry. On days like that, the crying just never seemed to end. I couldn't explain it. And I remember once, literally leaning on the counter, and crying with body-wracking sobs.

And I thought, "Woman, you have to learn to talk to yourself." Suddenly, there's two of me.

So I soothingly said to myself, out loud, "Okay, okay, no no no no. No no no, sh sh sh shhh."

"I don't know what I'm doing here, I'm scared, I don't know, I'm scared."

"Okay, okay, okay, sh sh sh sh, come on now, sh sh sh sh. Okay, think now, what did you do the last time you felt like this?"

"I don't remember."

More sternly. "Okay now, think. Now, come on."

"I went to a movie."

"Okay, good, get your coat."

"I don't want to go to a—"

"*Get your coat!*"

"Don't yell at me!"

"Come on, get in the truck."

"I don't know, I, I, I..."

"Open your eyes."

"I, I, I..."

So "we" get to the little cinema in the town, which has got like three tiny screens, and there's always one screen offering *Gone with the Wind*. I'm standing there looking at the posters, and it's, like, "There's nothing here, there's nothing here to see."

"Okay, I don't care what you see. You're going to see something. I don't give a *shit* what it is. Let's see, what's happening, what's happening, what's this, now, what's this here? Is this a Disney movie? Ah. Who likes a Disney movie?"

"I, I, I like a Disney movie."

"Oh, now, what's this one called? *Operation Dumbo Drop*!?"

Go inside, it's Friday night, there's three people there, they've been there since Wednesday. I get my popcorn. I sit down, and the warm bag of popcorn somehow comforts me. *Operation Dumbo Drop* is a Disney film, with men like Ray Liotta, a good actor, Danny Glover, somebody else, and an elephant. The room goes black, and the movie starts.

"Oh, my God! Oh, my God, it's a stupid movie! It's a stupid movie! Holy fuck, look at this! Oh, Danny, Danny! Aw, no, Ray, Ray!"

You know, I'm driving home picking my teeth, I'm thinking, as badly as I felt for myself, I feel way worse for Ray Liotta.

At home, I would watch the wood stove. I can watch fire for hours. I am a friend of fire, I'd like to say. I have watched fire for days. Fire is endlessly fascinating to me. You can open it up, and you can watch it, and it can be hotter or colder, hot, cold, hot, and then you can close it and you can play with the flue. More air, less air, more air, less air. And then sometimes you can open it and fritter stuff in it that doesn't belong there, but it burns really interestingly.

One time— I'd fall asleep in front of the fire a lot— I remember waking up and seeing that the fire had died down, so I opened it up, and I threw in more logs, I flat-palmed the door, and I closed it.

I burnt my whole palm.

Now, it's rare you do that kind of damage. And so I looked at it.

The first thing I did was laugh, and then it went pink and shiny, like I could see myself in my own palm.

"Quick, look at the time, what time is it? It's midnight. Now, look out the window, quickly now, and see if they built a hospital! Okay, now, Sandra, think."

By now, it's like I can feel my heart beating in my hand. Voice of reason:

"Okay, think now, come on, now, think."

"Okay, bag of ice? Ice is good."

"Okay, yeah, but you can't live with a bag of ice on your hand."

"No, no, okay."

"Come on now, think."

"I don't know. Um, aloe vera."

"Yeah, we're going to fly to fuckin' Hawaii! Come on! Think!"

So I run to the bathroom. In the bathroom, there's a basket of stuff I got when I cleaned out the medicine cabinet in the city, and I'm just rifling through it. Nothing. Nothing. Nothing. Finally, I find, at the bottom, a little tube of Anusol Plus hemorrhoid preparation. It says right on it: it cures burning, itching, and swelling. I got two out of three! So I squeezed half the tube onto my hand. Killed the pain dead. Killed the pain. I was so impressed— I put it on fuckin' everything now.

And that was a very important experience for me to have. It taught me in that moment that I will be creative in a crisis on my own behalf. Meaning, I am coming on my own side, which was such good news. So I was developing some confidence, and I felt ready for company.

So I got some kittens. Two little kittens. They were the size of oranges when I got them. They were so small, and I just wanted to crush their tiny little heads. When the kittens came into the house, the floor became An Amazing Entertainment Centre. I could watch the kittens for hours! And when I was tired of watching the kittens, I'd watch the wood stove!

Well, it was like having two channels!

Everybody has a recipe for healing. And they'll share their recipe for healing with you, even without you asking.

Some people say, "Oh, it takes a month for every year."

I don't know where they come up with these equations, by the way. I'm just sharing them with you.

And I said, "Well, we were together nine years, so nine months."

Somebody says, "No, no, no, no. You've got to go through the whole year, all the anniversaries, all the birthdays, you've got to go through the whole thing."

The truth is, it takes the time it takes. And only you know. And if anybody is rushing you, or telling you to hurry up, and that's just life and get on with it, then tell them to fuck off. And you can tell them I told you to tell them to fuck off. Because, that's not about you, they're not worried about you, they're just uncomfortable with you.

Now, if you are healing, you have to be honest to it. You have to honour it. You see, I had never felt so vulnerable, and so loved.

And I thought, well, "If I start healing and getting my feet underneath me a little bit, does that mean that they're not going to love me the same?"

And of course, that's not true. They love me the same, just not so intensively. When you start healing, it gives everybody else the chance to go home and have a life! So, ultimately, healing is what everybody wants you to do, and that's what you should want for yourself. It was actually Ray who taught me the phrase, "Pity pot."

I said, "What's that?"

He said, "Oh, you know the pity pot. You can't stay in the pity pot forever."

"I'm not in the pity pot! I'll have you know I'm far away from the pity pot! Not in the pity pot."

Okay, so that year, I could hear Christmas coming. Christmas was coming, and there isn't anywhere in the world you can go to get away from Christmas.

You know, you can go spelunking in the deepest cave on the planet, and you'll still hear "Jingle bells, jingle bells, jingle all the way." So, that year, man, I saw Christmas coming like a runaway train, and then it hit me like a ton of bricks. I wobbled, but I did not fall down. And my gift to me that Christmas was the knowledge that it takes a lot to kill me.

After Christmas and New Year's, I just thought, you know, I need to take a vacation. I just need to relax. Yes, I'm entirely too stressed, so I just lay in front of the wood stove like boneless chicken mostly, and then the kittens would come and find a spot, and do that thing, you know, like they tenderize you first, you know. And I'm lying there, thinking, "Oh, man, I'm losing so much muscle, oh, man. Maybe I should exercise. Oh, maybe I should sleep on that." You know, I woke up from that nap and the kittens were bigger.

I thought, you know, if I had a dog, I'd walk the dog. I've never had a dog. So I started looking through a local publication called *The Penny Saver*. Does anybody here know about *The Penny Saver*? Well, *The Penny Saver*, for those of you who don't know, is like a little newspaper, and it's delivered, and you can buy and sell anything in *The Penny Saver*. In fact, *The Penny Saver* that comes to the end of my road in my mailbox, actually has a Singles Classified. Some of the ads read like this:

"I am clean."

Why, you sweet-talking bastard, you!

So I'm looking in *The Penny Saver*, and there's a little teeny ad, and it says, "Fluffy puppies."

"Ohhhhh... flufffy puppppppiess!"

I call her up, and sure enough, she's a neighbour. In the country, anyone within the detonation area of a nuclear device is a neighbour. So I drove the half day to her home. I got there, she opened the basement door, and, poof! Six of the fluffiest puppies. Okay, there were three boys, and they were just like balls of fur! Balls! They had little squinty eyes and stumpy wiener legs sticking straight out of their bodies, not even touching the ground, like oars out of water, yelping, "Help me, help me, help me," like that, and the girl puppies were leaner, more coy, like, "Hello, are you chasing me? Then come along, yes, come along."

So I got the biggest female. She's a Husky-Shepherd-Satan cross. I brought her home, and I had a little crate for her, I put her in her crate, and she made the little wolf-shape with her body, and she howled, all night long!

She's keening for her people!

I said, "You know, you've come into a house of misery, cry along with me!"

God! I got about eight seconds' sleep. I dreamt her name: Chia. Chia Pet.

Now, a dog is not a cat. Let me try to explain. The kittens are quiet, quiet, and independent, and soft. And the puppy wants every minute of your attention, every ounce of your energy, twenty-four hours a day. And talk about energy. Every fuckin' day, I had to get up and put on my hat and my pants, my coat and my boots— I had to wear every garment I owned so I could walk this fuzzy loaf of bread the perimeter of a hundred and twenty-three acres, and she never tired, 'cause she's a Husky!

She kept up the whole way, "Are we in the Arctic yet?"

So, one time, I'm walking the dog. I will just tell you how it was, 'cause I still don't understand; I'll just tell you what would happen. I would walk the dog on the land, and the land is uneven, so I'm pitching and twitching, and stumbling around, trying to get my balance, right? And as I'm walking, I would start to get angry. I don't understand, like, gross motor activity leads to gross emotional activity, possibly? So as I'm walking, I'm getting angry, I'm getting angry, it's crawling up my body from the bottom up, and when it hits my stomach, it just mixes with something, and it turns into *rage*. And now I'm screaming; and I am mad at him, and I am mad at me, and I miss him, and I never want to see him again, I love him and I hate him and I like what happened but I didn't like how it happened, and I'm screaming and fuckin' pitching around.

Imagine driving by that.

I'm out of control, and I know it, I'm out of control, and I can feel the heat licking off me in arcs over my head, and I know I'm out of control, so I want to control something.

So: "Come here, puppy!"

Puppy goes, "No, I don't think so, you crazy fuck."

So I grab for the dog, and she thinks it's a game, so she squirts over there, and I'm trying to get her, and she's really fast, and now I'm rolling around in the dirt, screaming, and she thinks this is fun, and she jumps in the burrs. She comes out with all these fuzzy brown things, "What are these?! Do you like 'em, Mom, 'cause I got a whole bunch of them on my ass!" She's looking up at me, and I have to laugh, must laugh, because, you know God's in heaven, looking down, going, "Everybody, come here. Look at this! Someone remind me to make more of those fuzzy things!"

I knew it was time for me to be with my own kind, so I took Ladies' Adult Skate. I can skate! I just can't stop. So every Sunday I would show up at the Memorial Arena at one o'clock for Ladies' Adult Skate. I was the oldest woman there at thirty-eight, and the only one in the arena who had never had a child. That included the gay men, do you understand. They were all crowded around me going:

"So you, you, so you never had a child?"

"Not to my knowledge. I think I'd remember something like that."

And I had to ask myself why I never had children, really. And the truth is, whatever prompts a woman to want children never happened to me. I never got the call.

Maybe I got the call, and I was out.

I took a pottery course. I made two bowls: $127.50. The cats eat out of them. Oh, nothing's too good for my cats! Oh, and I was invited to join a garden club. I'm a gardener; I gardened in Toronto. One of the reasons to buy the farm was so I could blow my brains out gardening. But, man, you have no idea how big an acre is until you see the size of your spade. I gardened in downtown Toronto, when I lived there, and gardening in Toronto is not like gardening anywhere on the planet, certainly not the kind of gardening you're ever going to see on *Martha Stewart*:

"When I'm picking used condoms out of *my* front yard, I like to use a long barbecue tong. It's a good thing. Let's re-use those syringes, and make a festive wreath for the door."

So I was privileged to be asked to join this garden club, and I got to meet some women in my neighbourhood, and I was invited into their homes, these beautiful homes, to see what they've done with their country homes. Their gardens were magnificent. I mean, these women have forgotten more about gardening than I will ever know, and they're also the baking-est gals you'll ever meet. Oh, man, they bake your head right off. "Bring me your head, I'll bake it off." And it was at garden club I was introduced to bars, or squares— you know, sweet squares, with names. The first ones I encountered were "Hello Dollies." Do you know? I did not know. I don't know, it's a square, and it's square, and I'm at the garden club, at the buffet, with the coffee and the three-tiered plate thing. Yeah, you know it, right, with the different offerings on every tier?

So, I'm standing there, and the hostess says, "Sandra, have you tried the Hello Dollies?"

And she gestures to the plate, and I take one, and eat it. "Okay... *Hello Dolly*! Shit. These are good."

I spread my arms out on either side, keeping the other women away, and proceeded to eat the rest of them.

The other one is "Sex-in-a-Pan." Yeah? For those of you who do not know: pan, shortbread bottom, and then layers of sweet thing, sweet thing, sweet thing, sweet thing, sweet thing, and then white sweet thing on top. "Sex-in-a-Pan."

She came into garden club, looking like a librarian, a little dress with a little scarf tied to the side of her neck, her hair in a bun, holding the pan, and she said, "Sandra, have you tried the Sex-in-a-Pan?"

"Well, I shouldn't." I almost climbed into her lap.

I was told later by an Anglican minister's wife that you can make it with or without nuts.

It was at garden club that I had the good luck of

meeting a woman in my neighbourhood named Audrey. Audrey is in her middle eighties, and is a force of nature. She is an astonishment. And as a way of greeting me to the community, she invited me to her home. I was so honoured, really, and so I went there for tea and scones. It was so great.

We sat down, and she says, "Now, Sandra, how do you like living in the country? So quiet. So private."

I nod.

She said, "Oh, but you know, dear, I'm worried for you, I'm worried that you'll be lonesome. So, my recommendation is to accept *all* invitations. Oh, because you never know, dear. They may not come around again."

You got that right.

So whatever came my way, I was there!

"Highland Fling in Fergus?! What time's the caber toss?"

"Monster-Mudder Truck Rally, Skydome?! Pick me up at five!"

That February I was invited to the Millcroft Inn, for the "How to Attract Butterflies to Your Garden" seminar. When I got there, I met all the other fabulous women in my neighbourhood, and once we figured out how to attract butterflies to our gardens, we figured out how to attract alcohol to our table!

So now I was starting to know folk, and I'd see them on the road, and I'd wave.

I figured I'd earned my stripes with the half-ton and the six-hundred-and-sixty pounds of sand in the back, I'd fuckin' done that, man, so I decided to get something four-wheel drive. I decided I needed something with a back seat. I needed it covered at the back so I could carry the dog. I just needed this vehicle, and the only one that turned my head, and still the only one that turns my head, is called a Yukon. A Yukon is a Sports Utility Vehicle. They used to be called "trucks." Now they're called chi-chi poo-poo Sports Utility Vehicles. Like a woman, I go and get all the information. Like a woman, I read it all, and like a woman I remember all the information, and I start going to car lots that spring to look at the new Yukons.

When I get to the first car lot, the guy meets me in the yard.

He says, "So, you and your husband are looking for a new truck!"

That word was like a punch in the stomach.

"Uh, uh, I, no, I think my husband is looking for something else. I think it rhymes with truck, though."

The second place I went, I didn't park in the yard. I, actually, like, snuck into the yard. I was actually looking into the vehicle when the guy came up from behind me, and says,

"Hey, what's a little lady like you gonna do with all that truck?"

Startled, I said, "Well, I, I, I live on a farm, on a dirt road."

"Oh, living on a farm, eh?" Suddenly he's rocking back and forth on his heels, lecherously licking his chops. "Yeah, I might have to come by for breakfast some mornin'."

"Oh, yeah, that'd be *swell*! How do you like your sausage?"

Last place I went to, it was a beautiful spring day, and all the guys were standing outside having a smoke. They're all standing in a circle, and there's plumes of smoke coming out of the centre. It looked like they were picking a Pope.

I said, "Hi. Is anybody busy?"

"No."

Still no action.

"Well, I'm here to look at a Yukon."

And he gestures, "Yeah, there's some over there."

I said, "Well, okay, I'm looking for, like, a black Yukon, two-door."

He says, "Well, uh, there's a green one over there, four-door."

"Okay, green isn't black, four isn't two, hello!"

He says, "You know what we'll do? I'll take you inside, we'll do some paperwork, and I'll put you on the computer."

I said, "Well, you know, it's not my first day at the rodeo. I actually know what that means. That I sign something and then I'm beholden to buy whatever you find me."

"Awwww, come on, now. I don't mean to insult you, eh, but you've gotta trust me."

I said, "I don't mean to insult you, *eh*, but you're a *car salesman*."

He hung his head. He turned bright red. He went, "Good one!"

I asked my neighbour, Dan. Now Dan drives a Toyota Land Cruiser. I didn't even know Toyota had a 4 X 4, so I called a dealership in Toronto, and I said,

"Listen, I've just found out about the Land Cruiser. Give me some information."

He says, with a slow, arrogant drawl, "Yes... yes... we have a Land Cruiser on the lot, at present."

"Well, okay, go with that, Sparky. I mean, what's the big deal?"

He says, in a monastic tone, "You realize the Land Cruiser retails for $79,000?"

I said, "Yeah, so, what colour is it?"

He says, "White."

"Oh. Thank you for your time."

He says, "I beg your pardon?"

"I can't drive a white truck."

He says, "May I ask why *not*?"

I said, "White isn't slimming."

I said, "Dan, you gotta help me, man, I'm dying out there."

Dan says, "Sandra, you want to know Bob. Talk to Bob."

So I go.

Bob's a gentleman, offers me a chair and a fine cup of showroom coffee. We sit and talk trucks. He admires my knowledge of the vehicle.

He says, "But Sandra, what can *I* do for you?"

I said, "Bob, you've got to find me this thing. I'm

craving the vehicle. I've never craved a vehicle like this in my life. I have to have it, it's like, I think, maybe, a mid-life thing, but I don't care, I don't care, I want it! And it's got to be black."

He says, "Now, you don't want black in the country."

I said, "Don't you tell me what I want. I want black, and it has to be two-door, it has to be, like, loaded, I mean loaded, like, puking options, like, like, vomiting accessories. How many power-packages can you shove into this fucking thing?"

He's just smiling. "Oh, Sandra, we're going to get you that truck!"

Hallelujah, Bob!

They find me one, they bring it in, I go down to do the paperwork.

We sit down.

He starts asking, "Name. Telephone Number. Occupation."

I've done this, I know how to do this. I'm the only one who has to say my occupation with a straight face, by the way.

"Comedian."

He starts laughing so hard, I thought we were gonna lose him, like, honestly, he's like laughing,

laughing, at one point he puts his hand up as if to stop me...

He says, "Sandra, in thirty years, that's the best one yet!"

"No, Bob, that's what I do."

He says, straightening up, "Well, what are you, some kind of Seinfeld?"

I said, "No, I don't do TV. I perform in theatres, and if people come, and people laugh, then I'm a comedian, and if they don't, I'm a dramatist."

He sobers up, and just looks at me. "Well, can you give me an idea of what your income was last year?"

I said, "Well, you know, Bob, here's where it gets funny." I said, "I didn't work last year."

And his face just goes stone. Like, why are you yanking my chain? Obviously, I'm telling the man I'm a performer, and I didn't work last year. Good! And I see I'm losing him.

"But, Bob! Bob, come back, Bob! I have a GMAC financing history, Bob, Bob, I do have a mortgage, I must have a credit rating somewhere in the world, Bob!"

He looks at me, he's like, "Do you even have a credit card?"

"Yeah. I only have one, it's this Platinum American Express."

He looks at it. He goes, "How'd you get *this*?"

I said, "I was invited."

That's all he put on it. He put, "GMAC financing, Plat AMEX."

He stood up, sober as a judge, and he said, "Sandra, we're going to put 'er in like this, see how she goes." I drove away, and my Yukon is still in the yard!

I go home, I sleep. I get a call the next day.

"Sandra, it's Bob."

"Bob! Did they reject me?"

He says, "No! They told me, 'Give that woman anything she wants!'"

I said, "You know, Bob, if we could all keep that at the forefront of our minds..."

I got my Yukon. It totally rocks.

It's so great, that summer I just bought a bullet belt and put lipsticks in it! Yee-hah!

I got a phone call that spring from the Women's Television Network.

They called me up, and she says, "Sandra Shaymas?"

I said, "It's actually Sha-mas."

She says, "Oh. Well, I've always said Shay-mas."

"Oh, well, then. Pardon me. My mistake," I said. "What can I do for you?"

She says, "I'm calling from the Women's Television Network, and we're going to be doing a series of half-hour conversations, and we were wondering if you'd like to participate?"

I said, "What are the topics?"

She said, "Well, here's one you might enjoy: Sports Utility Vehicles— The New Bullies on the Road."

Amen. Where's the conversation in that?

I said, "And who the hell thinks of these things, anyway? I mean, who thought of that?"

She said, "Well, one of our producers, who drives a Mazda Miata, says that women who purchase Sports Utility Vehicles are simply expressing their anger and their repressed male rage!"

I smile. "Aw, you say it like it's a bad thing!" I said, "I am not going on TV and defending a purchase, that's just stupid."

She said, "But I understand you bought your vehicle 'cause you live on a farm."

I said, "Yeah, I live on a farm. I live on a farm, I have a dirt road, I like the four-wheel drive, I like the back seat, I like everything, but, let's face it, it's a man magnet."

She said, stunned, "Men are attracted to it?"

I went, "Duuhhh!"

She said, "But why?"

I said, "'Cause it's a big, big truck! It's got big, big wheels." I said, "It's got three ton of Detroit steel, it's got a big 350 under the hood, and a 120-litre gas tank."

And I spend a lot of time at the pumps. I've been gassing up and guys come over and watch the numbers turn over.

Snort. "Oh, she's thirsty, eh?"

Yes.

That spring I got a phone call from my neighbour, Natalie. She's eight years old. Natalie called, and she said, "Would you please be the Assistant Coach for our girls' soccer team?"

I said, "Put your mother on."

I said, "What's the story?"

She said, "Well, they need an Assistant Coach."

I said, "You know, I've never played soccer. I've never played a team sport, honestly. I'm not a team player. Hello."

She said, "Sandra, it's just Assistant Coach. All you have to know is how to cut an orange."

Accept all invitations!

"Put me down! I'll buy oranges, I'll practise at home!"

Within three days of that call I got a phone call from the league. Due to the magic of attrition, I have become a Coach.

"No no no no, no no no no no... 'cause the Coach *knows* something! I know *nothing*!"

She says, "Oh, for heaven's sakes, they're girls under eight, just have fun!" Click!

So, I meet my team. They're eight years old, and astonishing. They're all sucking on their hair, or trying to, and I meet them, and I say, "Guys, c'mere, okay, listen, honest and for true, I do not know how to play soccer. I have never played soccer, and the only reason I'm a coach is I'm taller, and I drive. Does anybody here know how to play soccer?"

Sadie puts up her hand.

I go, "Yeah, Sadie."

She goes, "Like, 'cause we're only eight, there's

just half a field, and there's three forwards, and three defence, and there's a goalie."

"Okay. How are we with that? Good, then let's have lunch."

So that summer I coached girls-under-eight soccer on a platform of Poise and Congeniality.

Standing on the sidelines, cigarette in a holder, with a slight British accent, yelling, "Run, babies, run! Danielle! Fab earrings! Play forward for a while, darling."

At the end of the summer, we weren't at the top, but we were not at the bottom. They were an excellent little team. The guy who coached the top team, he was a mess! He would yell at his team the whole time.

And all the tendons in his neck were sticking out; he looked like he was going to stroke out at any second. He scared me.

"Babies, come to me quickly. We're playing that maniac again. I say we forfeit and go to Dairy Queen."

It was one of the best summers of my life.

So now a whole year, actually more than a year, had gone by since May Day, and I took stock. I was up in an airplane— I was invited to go for a ride in an airplane over my land, and I saw my house, and my barn, and the road, and I saw the edge of my land.

And then what I saw was that my land touches other land that touches other land that touches other land that wraps right around the planet. And I realized that I have never been alone. For as much as I *felt* alone, I had never *been* alone. It was only my perspective that made me feel that way. On a greater scale, I'm on the same planet as everybody else. And I realized that the feeling of banishment from the city was actually a shove towards the welcoming arms of community.

I am a neighbour, I am a neighbour to others and others are neighbours to me. We look out for each other. When I see them on the road, we actually stop our vehicles, roll down our windows, and talk to one another. They know me, I know them, their children know me, they know my dog, and they bring her back all the time. You know, every time they bring her home, they say:

"Oh, a Husky wanders."

Maybe she won't wander with an anvil around her neck!

Then I realize it'd just make her stronger.

The dark that I was so terrified of is actually a luxury. It's the only way you can see stars. The quiet is a gift. I got to see me brave.

Now, "brave" doesn't feel brave when you're doing it, "brave" feels like shit when you're doing it. You only get to see "brave" after you've felt like shit. So, if you're feeling like shit, you're probably on your way to "brave."

I got to see me strong. I'm strong, I am brave, I am strong, I can split wood, I just got a better axe, frankly. And I got to do something very difficult in a relentlessly beautiful place. It's a privilege to live where I live. I know that. And the fact that you're here allows me to live there a little longer.

So, that summer, I was invited to a ladies' lunch in the city, so I put on my black, with the black and the black, and I was driving a black vehicle, so it just brought it all together.

And we sat down. Pam said to me, "Can you even think about where you were last year at this time?"

I said, "Yeah, wasn't I the one with the fire extinguisher around my neck? Yeah. I was like, a mess."

She said, "You know, I am so proud of you."

"Well, Pam, I couldn't have done it without you, you know."

She says, "No, no, I didn't move to the middle of fuckin' nowhere. You did that all by yourself."

"Anyway, thanks, Pam, thanks."

She said, "You know, you might want to think about seeing people."

"I see you, Pam."

She said, "No, you know what I mean. Dating."

"Why, Pam, this is so sudden!"

She said, "Not me, you idiot! You should start seeing men."

"Pam, Pam, that's not my best topic, Pam, can we, like, just talk about lunch?"

"No. No, we're gonna talk about *this*."

"I'm not, I'm not so good with this, Pam."

She said, "I don't see why not, you're interesting, you're attractive, you've got a lake."

"What the hell does the lake have to do with it?!"

She said, "Men like a lake."

I said, "Oh, I can date during fishing season? How refreshing is that?"

She said, "Now, I want you to think about this."

"Yes, Pam."

I'm driving home, thinking about our conversation, thinking, "Oh, mannnn," trying to compose my ad for *The Penny Saver*:

Woman with lake...

...seeks man with a lure.

You know, I thought, I have not even fished for fish! I should start small.

I found out that you have to have a license. So, I drove the hour to the convenience store, which is also the bait and tackle shop and finishing school. I filled out my application form for a fishing license, I paid my money, and then promptly forgot about it. I got a phone call about a month and a half later:

"Uh, Sandra Shay-mas?"

I said, "It's Sha-mas, actually. Speaking."

"It's Doug. Ministry of Natural Resources."

I said, "Hey, Doug, how are ya doing?"

"Oh, fine, thanks. Yourself?"

"Well, you know, I can't complain, nobody'd listen."

"Yeah, yeah, yeah, yeah, yeah... Yeah, yeah, yeah, yeah."

"Doug, what can I do for you?"

"Well, perhaps you have realized you have not received your fishing license as yet."

I said, "Geez, Doug, you're good."

He said, "That's on account of you did not fill out your application form correctly."

I said, "What'd I do, Doug, misspell my *name*?"

He says, "Oh, no. Where it says, 'Height,' you put '5,' and where it says 'Weight,' you put '6.'"

"I'm 5-6, Doug."

He said, "Oh, be that as it may, we do not have your weight."

"Are you telling me that I cannot *fish*, because you don't know how much I *weigh*?"

"Yeah, that is correct."

Beat. Beat. Beat.

"I weigh 350 pounds."

Got my license, 5-foot-6, 350 pounds.

My bookkeeper, Norma, said, "Sandra, that is a government document! You're going to get busted!"

I said, "I'll just tell them I went on an all-fish diet!"

Thank you very much. Good night!